W9-BVT-638

URGENCY EMERGENCY!

Itsy Bitsy Spider

For Sophie & James

Library of Congress Cataloging-in-Publication Data

Archer, Dosh, author, illustrator.
[Injured spider]
Itsy bitsy spider / Dosh Archer.
pages cm. — (Urgency emergency!)
First published in Great Britain in 2009 under the title: Injured spider.
Summary: "A spider arrives at City Hospital with some strange head injuries. How did this happen? And does it have anything to do with all the water rushing down the water spout?"—Provided by publisher.
ISBN 978-0-8075-8358-6 (hardback)
[1. Wounds and injuries—Fiction. 2. Medical care—Fiction. 3. Spiders—Fiction. 4. Animals—Fiction. 5. Characters in literature—Fiction. 6. Humorous stories.] I. Title.
PZ7.A6727Its 2013
[E]—dc23
2013005442

First published in Great Britain in 2009 by Bloomsbury Publishing Plc.
Published in 2013 by Albert Whitman & Company

Printed in China.
10 9 8 7 6 5 4 3 2 1 BP 18 17 16 15 14 13

For more information about Albert Whitman & Company, visit our web site at www.albertwhitman.com.

URGENCY EMERGENCY!

Itsy Bitsy Spider

Dosh Archer

Albert Whitman & Company
Chicago, Illinois

It was another busy day at City Hospital. Outside it was pouring rain. Doctor Glenda was making an important phone call and Nurse Percy was looking after one of the King's men, whose foot had been squashed by a huge egg.

Just then the ambulance arrived.

“Urgency Emergency!” called the Pengamedics. “We have an injured spider here. Injured spider coming through!”

Miss Muffet was running beside the trolley. She was the one who had called the ambulance.

"I don't know what happened," cried Miss Muffet. "I was just walking along when I found the spider lying in a puddle of water at the bottom of the waterspout.

I'm afraid of spiders, but I couldn't just leave her lying there."

“Step back!” cried Doctor Glenda. “Let me examine her.”

“It is just as I thought. She is very badly injured. There’s a cut on her head. Nurse Percy, put a bandage over that cut to stop any more bleeding.”

"Can you tell me your name?" asked Doctor Glenda as she shined a special light into the spider's eyes.

"Itsy Bitsy," said the spider.

“Good,” said Doctor Glenda. “How many fingers am I holding up?”

“Two,” said Itsy Bitsy.

“That’s right,” said Doctor Glenda. “You are in the hospital because you had some kind of accident. Can you tell us what happened?”

"I was just climbing up the waterspout," said Itsy. "Then it started to rain..."

"The last thing I remember is a big whoosh of water rushing toward me."

Doctor Glenda turned to Nurse Percy. "It looks like she was knocked down the waterspout by a downpour of rain. I think her brain is OK, but now we must act quickly—that cut will need stitches."

Itsy trembled with fear. Nurse Percy put an arm around her.

"Don't worry. It won't hurt a bit."

Nurse Percy gave Itsy a special injection to stop the stitches from hurting.

"I will do the stitches myself," said Doctor Glenda.

Nurse Percy brought the special needle and thread.

Very carefully Doctor Glenda made four tiny stitches to hold the cut together so that it could get better.

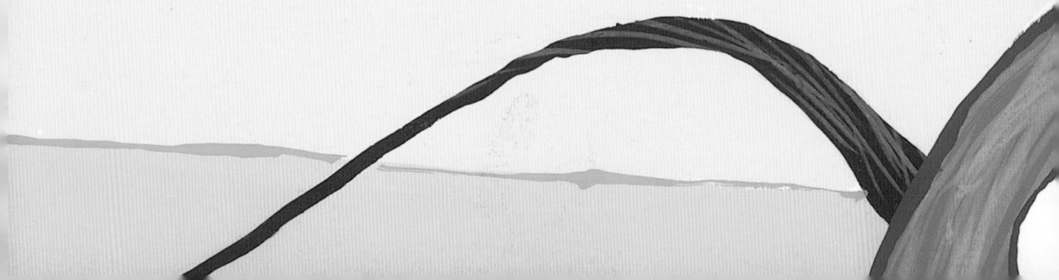

Nurse Percy held
all of Itsy's hands.

Nurse Percy was right—
it didn't hurt a bit.

Then he put a special sticky bandage on the cut to keep it nice and clean so it could heal.

But now Itsy was feeling a bit wobbly.

“Is there anyone who can help you get home?” asked Nurse Percy.

Itsy shook her head. “My sister is on vacation,” she said.

Nurse Percy had an idea.

He went to speak to Miss Muffet.

"I know you are afraid of spiders," said Nurse Percy, "but do you think you could overcome your fears and look after Itsy just for tonight? She will be feeling much better tomorrow."

Miss Muffet looked at poor Itsy.

"Oh, all right," she said. "Come on, Itsy. I don't have any flies for you to eat, but if you don't mind, you can have some of my curds and whey."

"I can never thank you enough," said Itsy Bitsy.

“All in a day’s work,” said Doctor Glenda.

Outside the sun had come out and dried up all the rain. Thanks to Doctor Glenda and her team, and with a little help from her new friend, Miss Muffet, Itsy Bitsy the spider would soon be climbing up that waterspout again.

Enjoy another funny beginning reader in the URGENCY EMERGENCY! series . . .

ISBN: 978-0-8075-8352-4
$12.99/$14.99 Canada

ALBERT WHITMAN & COMPANY
Publishing children's books since 1919
www.albertwhitman.com